S0-BSE-642

Forests

WITHDRAWN

LEMONT PUBLIC LIBRARY DISTRICT
50 East Wend Street
Lemont, IL 60439-6439

Forests

Joshua Rutten

THE CHILD'S WORLD®, INC.

Copyright © 1999 by The Child's World®, Inc.
All rights reserved. No part of this book may be
reproduced or utilized in any form or by any means
without written permission from the publisher.
Printed in the United States of America.

Library of Congress Cataloging-in-Publication Data
Rutten, Joshua.
Forests/ by Joshua Rutten.
p.   cm.
Includes index.
Summary: Describes the appearance, location,
and importance of forests and examines
the plants and animals that live in them.
ISBN 1-56766-486-5 (alk. paper)
1. Forest plants—Juvenile literature.
2. Forest animals—Juvenile literature
[1. Forest plants. 2. Forest animals. 3. Forests.]   I. Title.
QH86.R88   1998
578.73—dc21   97-36022
CIP
AC

Photo Credits

© Aldo Brando./Tony Stone Images: 26
© Charles Krebs/Tony Stone Images: cover
© Chris Cheadle/Tony Stone Images: 10
© Daniel J. Cox/Natural Exposures: 20
© 1994 Darrell Gulin/Dembinsky Photo Assoc. Inc: 29
© David N. Davis: 6, 15
© David Hanson/Tony Stone Images: 9
© 1994 Dominique Braud/Dembinsky Photo Assoc. Inc: 16
© 1997 Jim Nachel/Dembinsky Photo Assoc. Inc: 24
© Michael Busselle/Tony Stone Images: 30
© 1997 Rod Planck/Dembinsky Photo Assoc. Inc: 2
© 1993 Ron Goulet/Dembinsky Photo Assoc. Inc: 19
© Terry Donnelly/Tony Stone Images: 13
© Tom Tietz/Tony Stone Images: 23

On the cover...

Front cover: This huge forest in Washington is full of pine trees.
Page 2: This quiet forest in Michigan is very green.

3 1559 00105 1281

Table of Contents

If you travel away from the lights and noise of the big city, you might find yourself in a very different land. In this land, the air is cool and fresh. Huge trees tower high in the air. Everywhere you look you can see life. What type of place is this? It's a forest.

⇐ It is easy to see why forests are so beautiful.

If you were to fly over a forest, you would see thousands of treetops. In fact, the entire area would look like a giant green blanket! Trees are some of the most important plants on Earth. They give us clean air and shade us from the hot sun. Life would not be the same without trees.

This forest in Thailand is full of tall, green trees. ⇒

How Big Do Trees Grow?

Most forest trees grow to be about 25 feet tall. With lots of sunshine and rain, many can live for around 200 years. Some trees grow even bigger than others. California's *Sequoia* trees reach heights of over 360 feet! These trees are so big, the wood from one tree could build 50 houses.

Sequoia trees can live to be over 3,000 years old. That is a very long time, but one kind of tree can live even longer. The *bristlecone pine* can live for over 4,500 years. A tree that old started growing when the ancient Egyptians were building the pyramids!

⇐ Sequoias like this one grow very wide and tall.

Why Do Forests Have So Many Plants?

When you walk into the forest, you notice that the sun seems dim. As you look up, you see the forest **canopy**. The canopy is a layer of leaves and branches high above the ground. This layer is thick enough to keep the Sun's heat out of the forest. The canopy also keeps much of the forest's water from escaping into the air.

By keeping the forest shady and moist, the canopy makes the weather perfect for other plants to grow. In fact, the growing conditions are so good that over 1,000 **species**, or types, of plants can live in a single forest!

This canopy of branches keeps the forest below moist and cool. ⇒

Are There Different Kinds of Forests?

Just as there are different types of trees, there are different kinds of forests. The *coniferous forest* is made up of pine and fir trees. They stay green all year, even in winter. Coniferous forests cover much of the far north, where the bitter cold would kill other plants and trees.

Thousands of trees make up this coniferous forest. ⇒

Rain forests grow in warm, wet areas. Because the weather is warm all year, these forests are thick and green. Many different types of plants and animals live in rain forests. In fact, many rain forest plants and animals are found nowhere else in the world.

When most Americans picture a forest, they think of a *temperate forest*. In a temperate forest, the trees' leaves change color with the different seasons. The leaves are bright green in the spring and deep green in the summer. In the fall, they turn all kinds of bright colors. Then, in the winter, the trees lose their leaves. But why?

In the fall, the trees in this Michigan forest turn bright colors. ⇒

Why Do Trees Lose Their Leaves?

During the spring and summer, the forest is nice and warm. The trees spread their leaves to soak up the sun and the rain. To live through the cold winter, the trees shut down. They must stop the flow of water to their leaves. Without the water, the leaves dry up and fall off. All winter long, the trees stand bare. Then, when the spring sun warms the trees, new leaves begin to grow.

⇐ The trees in this forest have lost their leaves for the winter.

What Animals Live in Forests?

Forests are filled with much more than trees and plants. Thousands of animals live there as well. During the day, you can see birds of all sizes and colors flying and eating. Squirrels, rabbits, beaver, and deer live in forests, too.

Many forest animals are **nocturnal**, which means that they are active at night and sleep during the day. Raccoons, opossums, foxes, and skunks are all nocturnal forest animals. Mice, frogs, badgers, and bats also call the nighttime forest their home.

This young deer lives in a forest. ⇒

Why Are Forests Important?

Forests are important in many ways. They provide homes for most of the animals on Earth. Forest trees give us nuts and fruits to eat and wood for cooking and heating. We build our houses from wood. Even the paper in this book comes from wood!

Forests are also important because they protect the ground from washing or blowing away. This washing-away of soil is called **erosion**. The roots of the forest's trees keep the soil in place. Without forests, there would be terrible mudslides and dust storms that could destroy homes and crops.

Forests once covered most of the planet. They covered most of the United States and much of Europe. There were also beautiful forests in China and Japan. But over the years, people have destroyed many of the world's forests. Some were cut down so people could use their wood. Others were burned or bulldozed to make room for cities and roads. Today, there are fewer forests left.

⇐ People burned down this Colombian rain forest.

Are Forests in Danger?

As more and more forests are destroyed, the plants and animals that live in them disappear. To help save them, many governments have made forests into national parks. When a forest is made into a national park, its plants and animals are protected. No cities or freeways can be built in a national park.

This national park in California is quiet in the early morning. ⇒

But forests are still in danger. They are still being cut down to make room for buildings and farm fields. And fires and pollution damage even protected forests in parks. Every year, large areas of forest are destroyed when people are careless with fire. Even more forest land becomes damaged from pollution and waste. If we want to have our wonderful forests around for a long time, it is up to us to protect and care for them.

⇐ Thick, green forests like this one need to be protected.

Glossary

canopy (KAN–uh–pee)
The canopy is the layer of leaves and branches that form a roof over the forest. The canopy keeps the forest shady and moist.

erosion (ee–ROH–zhun)
Erosion is the washing or blowing away of soil. The roots of forests help prevent erosion.

nocturnal (nok–TUR–null)
Nocturnal animals come out only at night. Many animals that live in the forest are nocturnal.

species (SPEE–sheez)
A species is a separate type of animal or plant. Thousands of species of plants and animals live in forests.

Index